Santa Moves South

E. J. Sullivan

Illustrated by
Philomena O'Neill

SWEETWATER
PRESS

SWEETWATER
PRESS

Santa Moves South

Copyright © 2006 Sweetwater Press

Produced by Cliff Road Books

ISBN-13: 978-1-58173-546-8
ISBN-10: 1-58173-546-4

Printed in China

Santa Moves South

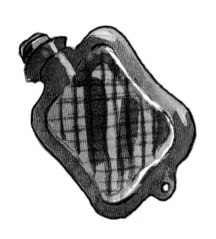

It was cold at the North Pole even in summer. Santa and Mrs. Claus were used to the ice and snow, of course. But there were times when Santa wished he lived somewhere else.

Santa couldn't help thinking about how much he enjoyed visiting all those children in the South on Christmas Eve.

This year was harder than ever on Santa. As he worked with his elves in the workshop, his fingers ached with cold. His back hurt. His feet were frozen.

He let out a big sigh after dinner. "I don't know how much more of this I can take," he said to Mrs. Claus. "I'm going to bed and not getting up until summer."

Mrs. Claus worried. What would the children do for Christmas if Santa wouldn't leave his warm bed? The next morning, she went online.

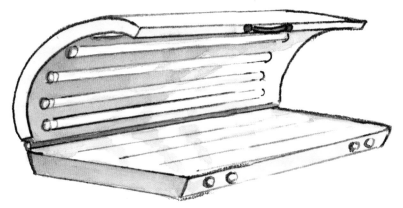

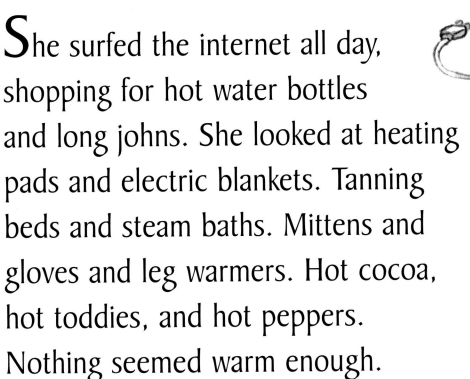

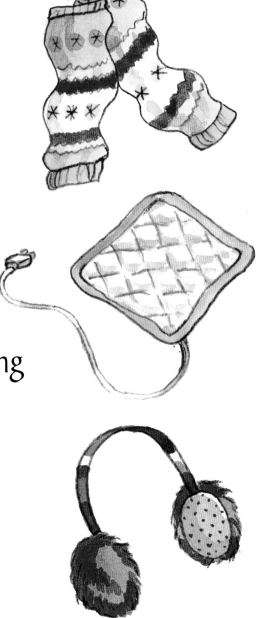

She surfed the internet all day, shopping for hot water bottles and long johns. She looked at heating pads and electric blankets. Tanning beds and steam baths. Mittens and gloves and leg warmers. Hot cocoa, hot toddies, and hot peppers. Nothing seemed warm enough.

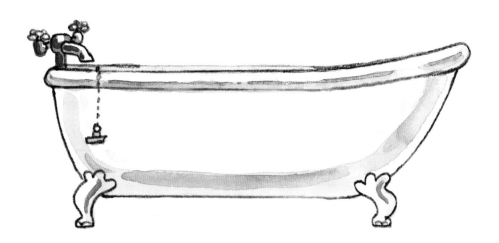

Then she decided
maybe Santa needed a tropical vacation.

But if Santa went away on vacation, no toys would be made. There would be no Christmas deliveries. And when Santa came back to the ice and snow, he might be colder and grouchier than ever.

Mrs. Claus felt like crying. She looked out the window at the reindeer shivering in the snow. Icicles dripped from their antlers. There was only one solution.

Mrs. Claus put a pot of soup on the stove for Santa.

She went out to the reindeer and hitched them to the sleigh. She told the elves to keep working. Then she flew away.

The elves were very worried, but they kept working, taking turns getting Santa his soup and putting more blankets on his bed. It was the coldest winter ever at the North Pole.

When Mrs. Claus got back on Christmas Eve, there was barely enough time to finish the toys and load them on the sleigh.

But together the elves did it. Then they all went to get Santa out of bed.

Mrs. Claus and the elves flew 'round the world with Santa, helping him make deliveries. Santa perked up as they headed South. "I have a surprise for you after we make our last stop," said Mrs. C.

Santa was still a little grouchy. But
he cheered up after the last delivery, as the
sleigh sailed over a hill and down into a cozy
valley filled with magnolia trees and live oaks.
There he saw a little house with greens in the
garden and camellias blooming by the fence.

Inside, some of the elves had a hot dinner waiting: fried chicken, sweet potatoes, corn bread, three kinds of veggies, sweet tea, and pecan pie for dessert.

Mrs. Claus opened a window
and a soft breeze came in.
"Welcome to the South,"
she said to Santa Claus.

"Don't worry," Mrs. Claus added as she helped put Santa's feet up. "I told the post office where to deliver your mail."